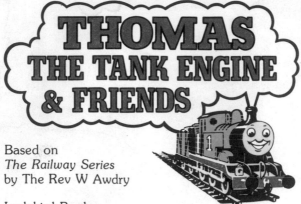

THOMAS THE TANK ENGINE & FRIENDS

Based on
The Railway Series
by The Rev W Awdry

Ladybird Books

Acknowledgment
Photographic stills by Kenny McArthur of Clearwater Features
for Britt Allcroft (Thomas) Ltd.

British Library Cataloguing in Publication Data
Awdry, W.
    Toby and the stout gentleman; Thomas in trouble.—
    (Thomas the tank engine & friends; 5)
    I. Title   II. Series
    823'.914[J]   PZ7
    ISBN 0-7214-0907-5

© WILLIAM HEINEMANN LTD 1984
© BRITT ALLCROFT (THOMAS) LTD 1984
© In presentation LADYBIRD BOOKS LTD MCMLXXXV
All rights reserved. No part of this publication may be reproduced, stored in a retrieval system, or transmitted in any form or by any means, electronic, mechanical, photo-copying, recording or otherwise, without the prior consent of the copyright owners.
Printed in England

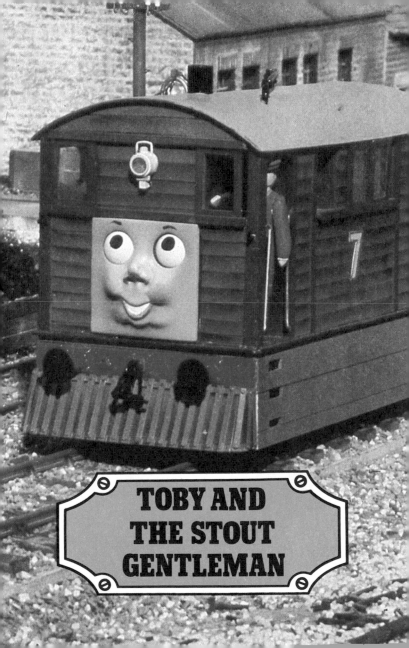

TOBY AND THE STOUT GENTLEMAN

Toby and the stout gentleman

Toby is a tram engine. He is short and sturdy. He has cow-catchers and side-plates and doesn't look like a steam engine at all.

Toby's tramline runs alongside roads and through fields and villages. He takes

trucks from farms and factories to the main line and he always rings his bell cheerfully to everyone he meets.

He has a coach called Henrietta who has seen better days. Toby is attached to Henrietta and always takes her with him.

"She might be useful one day," he says.

Henrietta used to have nine trucks rattling along behind her but now there are only three or four because the factories send their goods mostly by lorry.

The cars, buses and lorries often have accidents. Toby is always careful. He

hasn't had an accident for years. But the
buses are crowded and Henrietta is
empty.

"I can't understand it!" says Toby,
sadly.

People come to see Toby but they always laugh and stare. "Isn't he quaint and old-fashioned!" they say. They make Toby so cross.

One day a lady and a stout gentleman with a little girl and boy stood nearby. The gentleman looked important but nice. He was, of course, the Fat Controller but Toby didn't know this yet.

"Come on, Grandfather!" called the children. "Do look at this engine."

"That's a tram engine, Stephen," said the stout gentleman.

9

"Is it electric?" asked Bridget.
"Whoosh!" hissed Toby, crossly.

"Sh! Sh!" said her brother. "You've offended him."

"But trams *are* electric, aren't they?" asked Bridget.

"They are mostly," said the stout gentleman, "but this is a steam tram."

"May we go in it, Grandfather?" asked the children.

The guard had begun to blow his whistle.

"Stop!" shouted the stout gentleman. He raised his arm and they all scrambled into Henrietta.

"Hip, hip, hurray!" chanted Henrietta as she rattled along behind Toby.

But Toby did not sing. "Electric indeed!" he snorted. He was very hurt.

The stout gentleman and his family climbed out at the next station. "What's your name?" he asked.

"Toby, sir," said the tram engine.

"Thank you, Toby, for a very nice ride," said the stout gentleman.

"Thank *you*, sir!" said Toby, politely. He felt much better now. "This gentleman," he thought, "is a gentleman who knows how to speak to engines."

The children came every day for a fortnight to see Toby and Henrietta. Sometimes they rode with the guard and sometimes in the empty trucks.

On the last day of their holiday, the driver invited them into his cab.

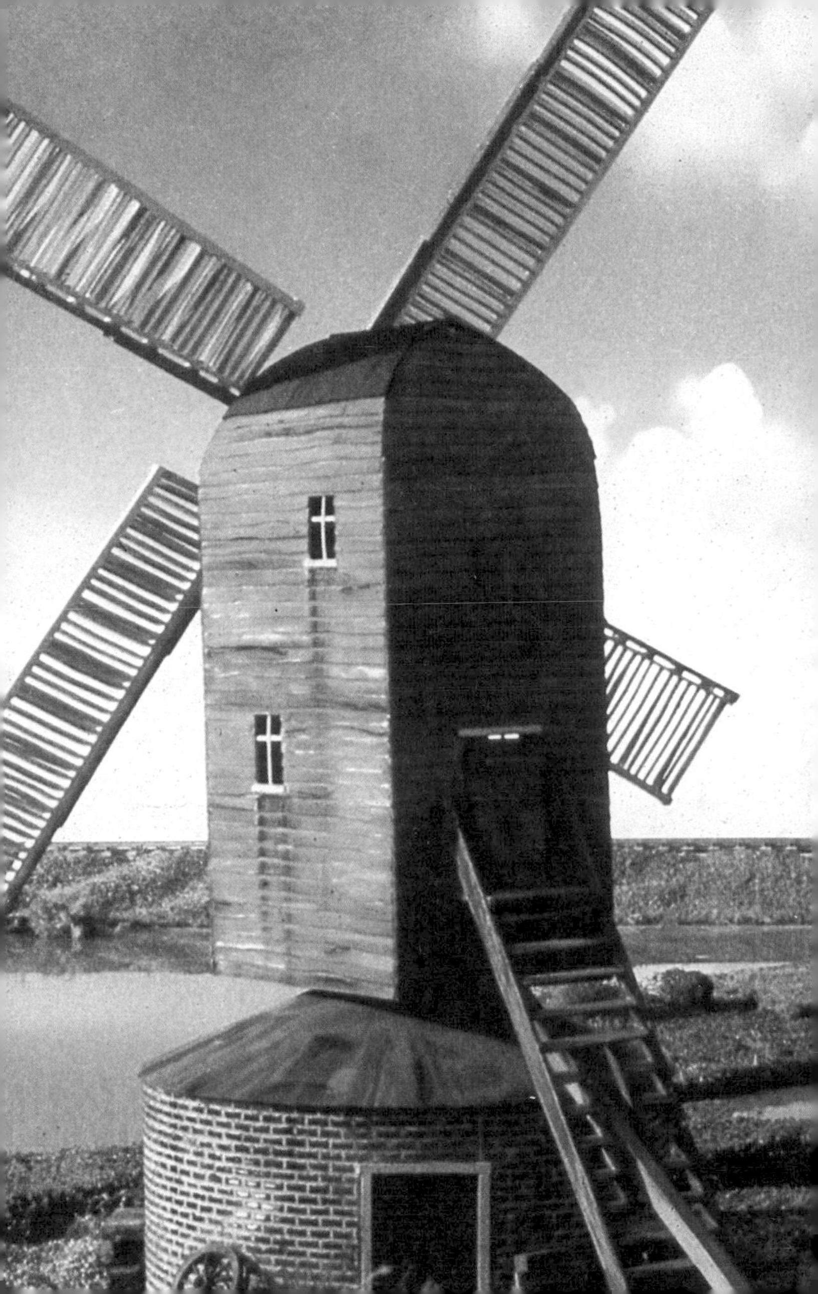

Everyone was very sorry when the
stout gentleman and his family had to go
away.

"Goodbye," said Bridget and Stephen
and they thanked Toby and his driver.

"Peep, pip, peep!" whistled Toby.
"Come again, soon!"

"We will, we will!" cried the children
and they waved until Toby was out of
sight.

The months passed. Toby had few trucks to pull and even fewer passengers travelled on his tramline.

"This is our last day, Toby," said his driver, sadly, one morning. "The Manager says that we must close the line."

That day everyone wanted the chance of a last ride with Toby and Henrietta.

Henrietta had more passengers than she could manage. They rode in the trucks and crowded into the brake van. The guard didn't have enough tickets to go round!

As they travelled along, the passengers joked and sang.

"Goodbye, Toby," said the passengers, afterwards. "We are very sorry that your line is closing down."

"So am I," said Toby, sadly.

The last passenger left the station and Toby puffed slowly to his shed. "Nobody wants me," Toby thought and he went unhappily to sleep.

Next morning the shed doors were
flung open and Toby woke with a start.
His driver was waving a piece of paper.
"Wake up, Toby!" he shouted. "Listen to
this. It's a letter from the stout
gentleman."

Toby listened and...
*But I mustn't tell you any more or I shall
spoil the next story.*

THOMAS IN TROUBLE

Thomas in trouble

There is a line to a quarry at the end
of Thomas's branch line. It goes for some
distance along by the road.

Thomas was always very careful there
in case anyone was coming. "Peep, pip,
peep!" he whistled, then people got out
of the way and he puffed slowly along,
with his trucks rumbling behind him.

Early one morning there was a policeman standing close to the line. Thomas liked policemen. He had been a great friend of the Constable who used to live in the village.

"Peep, peep! Good morning!" Thomas whistled.

Thomas expected that this new policeman would be as friendly as the other one. He was sorry to see that the policeman didn't look friendly at all.

The policeman was red in the face and very cross. "Disgraceful!" he spluttered.

"I didn't sleep a wink last night — it was *so* quiet."

The policeman looked at Thomas. "And now," he said, "engines come whistling suddenly behind me!"

"I'm sorry, sir," said Thomas. "I only said 'good morning' to you."

"Where is your cow-catcher?" he asked, sharply.

"But, I don't catch cows, sir" said
Thomas.

"Don't be funny!" snapped the
policeman. He looked at Thomas's
wheels. "No side plates, either!" he
muttered and he wrote in his notebook.

Then he spoke sternly to Thomas. "Engines going on public roads must have their wheels covered and a cow-catcher in front. You haven't so *you* are dangerous to the public."

"Rubbish!" said Thomas's driver. "We've been along here hundreds of times and there has never been an accident."

"That makes it worse," said the policeman. And he wrote 'REGULAR LAW BREAKER' in his book.

Thomas's driver climbed back into the cab and Thomas puffed sadly away.

The Fat Controller was having breakfast. He was eating toast and marmalade. His wife had just given him some more coffee.

The butler came in. "Excuse me, sir," he said. "You are wanted on the telephone."

"Bother that telephone!" said the Fat Controller.

"I am sorry, my dear," he said a few minutes later. "Thomas is in trouble with the police and I must go at once." He gulped down his coffee and hurried from the room.

At the station, Thomas's driver told the Fat Controller what had happened.

"Dangerous to the public indeed! We'll see about that!" said the Fat Controller.

The policeman came on to the platform and the Fat Controller spoke to him at once. But however much the Fat Controller argued with him...

...it was no good.

"The law is the law," said the policeman, "and we can't change it." The Fat Controller felt quite exhausted.

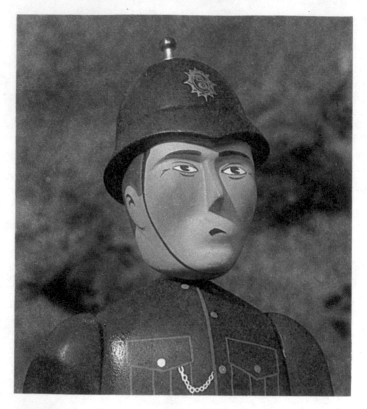

"I'm sorry," he said to Thomas's driver. "It's no use arguing with policemen. We will have to make those cow-catcher things for Thomas, I suppose."

"Everyone will laugh, sir," said Thomas, sadly. "They will say that I look like a tram."

The Fat Controller stared at Thomas and then he laughed. "Well done, Thomas! Why didn't I think of it before?" he said.

"We want a tram engine," he went on. "When I was on my holiday, I met a nice little engine called Toby. He hasn't enough work to do and he needs a change. I'll write to his Controller at once!"

A few days later Toby arrived.

"That's a good engine," said the Fat Controller. "I see that you have brought Henrietta with you."

"You don't mind, do you, sir?" asked Toby, anxiously. "The Station Master

wanted to use her as a hen house, and that would never do."

"No, indeed," said the Fat Controller, gravely. "We couldn't allow that!"

Toby made the trucks behave even better than Thomas did.

At first, Thomas was jealous, but he was so pleased when Toby rang his bell and made the policeman jump that they have been firm friends ever since.